A Child's Guide
to Common
Household Monsters

James Otis Thach

ILLUSTRATIONS BY David Udovic

FRONT STREET
Asheville, North Carolina

I guess you've always known it—that they live inside your home.
You've probably seen or heard them when you're sitting all alone.

Oh sure, you've tried to tell yourself, that must have been the cat.

And any breeze could make the upstairs hallway creak like that.

But now perhaps you're old enough to finally face the truth. ...

Your house is full of monsters, from the basement to the roof!

The first is very near-at-hand, just
There upon the hardwood floor

He shuffles through the dust and dark; he likes to watch your feet.
At times he'll steal a sock or two—that's all he likes to eat.
But why does he confine himself to such a narrow gloom?

He's hiding from the other monster lurking in your room!

The other monster in your room is easy to ignore,
though you may hear a muffled rustle through your closet door.

The closet monster feels at home amid your hanging clothes.
The smell of freshly laundered things is music to his nose.

He also has a fondness for your old forgotten toys,
and only when he drops one will he ever make a noise.

He'll never try to pounce on you
or shout or be dramatic—
for after all, he's hiding from
the monster in the attic!

Another monster makes his lonely home below your roof,
and if you've listened late at night, perhaps you've heard the proof.

He loves to go from box to box and keeps himself amused
with Christmas lights and dusty books and things you've never used.

Although he may seem scary, he's as timid as a mouse.
He's up there hiding from the monster underneath your house.

Way down in the basement
lives another creature still—
the one perhaps most likely to
inspire a little chill.

He hides among the spider webs
behind the washer-dryer
and warms his many hands
before the boiler's glowing fire.

You might not be so frightened by him if you only knew ...

the reason he's been hiding is, he's so afraid of ... you!

It's nice to know the monsters in your home are not a threat, but don't go rushing off to strike up friendships with them yet.

For if you do I promise you, the next time thunder rolls ...

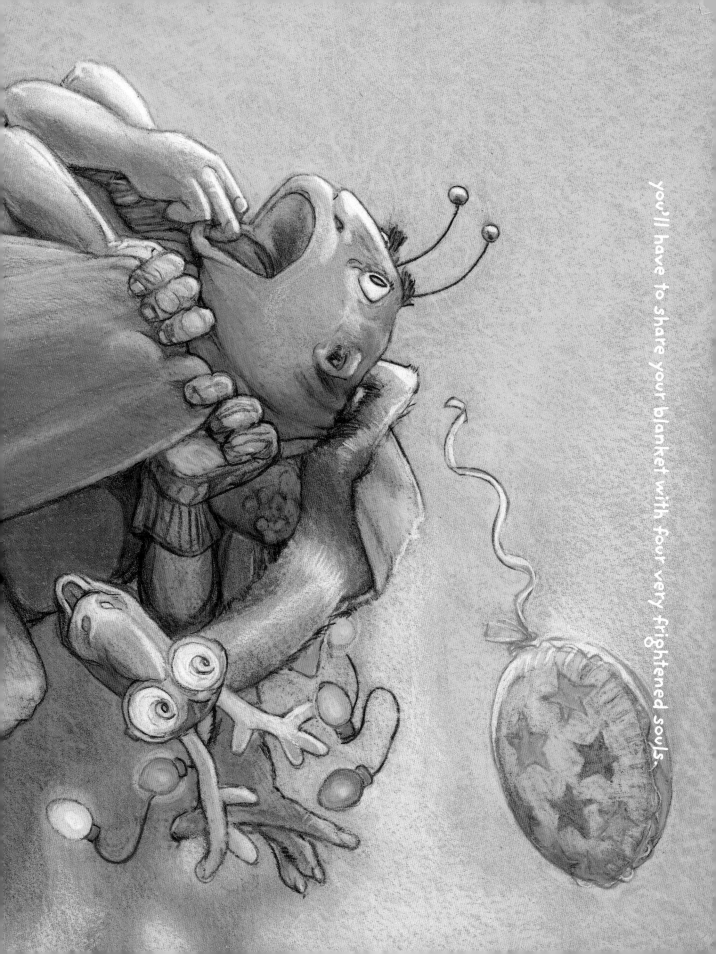

you'll have to share your blanket with four very frightened souls.

Text copyright © 2007 by James Otis Thach
Illustrations copyright © 2007 by David Udovic
All rights reserved
Printed in China
Designed by Helen Robinson
First edition

Library of Congress Cataloging-in-Publication Data

Thach, James Otis.
  A child's guide to common household monsters / James Otis Thach ;
illustrations by David Udovic. — 1st ed.
     p. cm.
  Summary: A girl discovers that her house is full of friendly monsters
who are more afraid of each other than she is of them.
  ISBN 978-1-932425-58-1 (hardcover : alk. paper)
  [1. Monsters—Fiction. 2. Stories in rhyme.] I. Udovic, David, ill. II. Title.
  PZ8.3.T2355Ch 2007
  [E]—dc22
                                    2006102549

FRONT STREET
An Imprint of Boyds Mills Press, Inc.
815 Church Street
Honesdale, Pennsylvania 18431